TIT TADA-THE UNLIKELY SEX BEAST

A ROMANCE ALONE NOVEL

© 2017 Urquhart **Randolph**

VISIT US
WWW.GLOFTON.COM
Enroll in our VIP list.
Be the first to be notified on our latest published book.
Downloading for free gifts.

Disclaimer

This is a work of fiction. Names, characters, organizations, spots, occasions and occurrences are either the results of the creator's creative energy or utilized as a part of an invented way. Any similarity to real people, living or dead, or genuine occasions is absolutely adventitious.

ISBN:
eBook: 978-1-946792-09-9
print:978-1-946792-10-5
audio/d :978-1-946792-11-2

Published by Glofton llc

TABLE CONTENT

THE GENESIS OF TROUBLES

CHAPTER 1

The night before, he'd lighted up their home with a disturbingly electrifying sorority party. Yes! He's got a knack for women. He stays with his parents at Denver and his name is James Stones. In the latter part of his life, he's widely known by his nickname that very few people know his real name.

Back in college, all his friends - or should I say most of them - were ladies. The guys usually made fun of him because he had feminine features. There were instances when gays made advances at him because he had the looks.

Eventually, he found pleasure in the company of ladies. Unlike his male counterparts who were either mocking him or making gay-advances towards him, the ladies showed him more attention, adored and worshipped him.

Before he left college, he was accepted into a sorority group and at that point, there was no turning back. He became a complete ladies' guy. They did almost everything together with him and even their nudity was not hidden from him. As time went on, he evolved from massaging to caressing, from caressing to kissing and fondling, and in the end sexing them became a norm.

As a matter of fact, the ladies lured him into it and the day he lost his virginity to Vicky, he said to himself, 'I'm never gonna stop doing this.' It was during those times that he was nick-named TIT TADA, derived from the words TITS and TOUCHER, which meant he was extremely skilled at fondling and caressing breasts. Tada was dating no one by then but was servicing any and every girl on campus who needed some satisfaction for their libido.

As for the ladies, they felt completely safe with him because they knew their sexual escapades with him were gonna remain discrete, unlike most of the other guys on campus who go public after almost every sexual bout.

They would tell their male friends about how she screamed, the frown or smile on her face, how she moaned and even the minutest of details. Worst of it all, some made secretly recorded sex tapes of them.

Tada became the go-to-guy for every lady. As a matter of fact, they were paying him money, giving him gifts and feeding him for free. They made him feel better and much adored than any other person, society or group had ever made him feel. To him, not even his parents' love could replace it.

After college, he organized an after-school party at home but it didn't turn out well with his parents. His father was a Bishop and his mom, a lady Pastor. They were a couple of such high reputation. They returned around 12 am on that fateful night only to see the children of Lucifer demonizing their home with fornication, lesbianism, drunkenness etc.

Making matters worse, they caught their only son in a threesome on their matrimonial bed. They boiled with rage, so much that they turned the party upside down - crashed the sound equipment, chased everyone out, and called in the police.

Since then, they had become very strict on James and their relationship with him was constantly deteriorating.

Two months afterwards, his parents had left town for a church program that would last two days but instead of joining them, James saw that as a perfect opportunity to do what he loved best. His birthday was two days away but his parents were gonna be away. They explained why they couldn't be around on his birthday but entreated him to be good. However, their intention was to surprise him — return on the night the program ends with a new car as his birthday present.

The church program ended by 8:30 pm, and their home was a two-hour drive away. They drove back home but upon arriving, around 10:45 pm, they saw James was at it again. He was having a birthday party but this time, it was much worse than the after-school party he'd organized two months ago. The highly respected religious couple could not bear it and reacted no differently from they did the other time. James was highly enraged. A battle of words ensued between him and them.

Having exhausted themselves with accusations and counteraccusations, James locked himself up in his room and made up his mind that he was gonna leave home in order to avoid all those boring religious restrictions.

The day after his twentieth birthday was a Saturday and at 7:30am, he stepped out of his room with two bags and began making his way towards the door. His mom who was coming out of the kitchen enthused, 'James, where are you going?' He put on a stern face however, refusing to answer her while hurrying to the door.

She cried out whiles racing towards him, 'James, come back! Come back here James!' She grabbed his arms, pleaded and tried wrestling the bags out of his hands. 'Please don't do this, we love you. Please James.'

Joel Stones, James' father who was by then in bed, could hear his wife's desperate sober pleas. He jumped out of bed, rushed out of his room, and made his way towards them. When James saw, him approaching, he pushed his mom to the ground in an attempt to hurry out of the house but his dad moved swiftly, grabbed him by the scruff of his neck, and dealt him a thunderous slap.

'Have you gone insane?' his dad queried.

'What do you want from me? I'm leaving you two old fools. I've got the right to my own free...'

His dad stopped him in the middle of his statement with a cruel slap. James, thinking he was now man enough, grabbed his dad and attempted wrestling him to the ground. It transpired into an early morning father-and-son combat. His father counteracted, overpowered him and threw him to the floor. He beat the crap out of him till his face was as swollen as a victim of wild beestings.

Although his mom tried so much to rescue him, Joel Stones was just too strong to be overpowered by his skinny feeble wife. After rebuking his son, Joel Stones got off him, grabbed the bags from the floor, and began heading towards James' room.

Before his father could leave his sight, he rose to his feet, reached for a pistol in his back pocket and then, POW! POW! He shot twice at his dad. The steel coated bullets went straight into him, piercing his left shoulder blade and left ribs. He hurriedly snatched the two bags from the palms of his fainting dad and raced off. The scared and confused woman rushed desperately to the aid of her husband.

'Call Doctor Charles,' Bishop Stones said. Doctor Charles was their family doctor as well as Joel Stones' best friend. The Bishop knew his son's future would be permanently ruined if the police were to get involved and since it's a hospital procedure to provide a police report for gunshot patients, Dr. Charles was the only one who could risk treating him without asking for a police report.

She phoned Doctor Charles who quickly arranged for an ambulance. In about six minutes, the ambulance was at their home and he was attended to. They placed him on a stretcher, fixed oxygen on him and sped off to Doctor Charles' hospital.

CHAPTER 2 -

A police vehicle approaches the house about 15minutes later in response to a concerned neighbor's call. They meet an empty house, search it and then head towards the alleged hospital – the neighbors had seen the name of the hospital on the ambulance.

Upon arrival of the ambulance, Bishop Joel Stones discusses with his wife that he called Dr. Charles because their son's crime has to be kept discrete from the police, that James' life will be ruined if the police found out.

Bishop Joel Stones' strength begins failing rapidly and they rush him to the hospital's intensive care unit. Dr. Charles and the other medics attend to him but he makes a last request to speak with his wife. They reject it initially but later allow them a minute because he insists.

He tells her that he'll probably die and the police would come interrogating her soon but contrary to what they had agreed, she should let out the truth. She cries upon hearing that but the medical team usher her out and attend to the Bishop.

They perform a surgery that lasts one and half hours but the Bishop falls into coma afterwards. She's saddened by the news. Moments later, the police request to get a statement from her but she's in no mood to do so for the time being.

Meanwhile, Tada who is on the run, arrives at Vicky's place. Vicky is the closest friend he had on campus, the girl who broke his virginity, and the very one who had introduced him to drugs in the latter days of college. He rings the bell and looks around to see if anyone is coming at him. She opens the door and sees Tada. She screams excitedly and hugs him but he's not excited. She helps pull his bags inside and shuts the door.

'Finally you came. I hope you're here to spend a month or two and not some days. You have no idea how I've missed you and been longing for that impossible dick of yours.'

She realizes Tada looks grumpy. Then she says, 'Look, I'm sorry I couldn't make it to the party yesterday. I was just caught up in some mess and I had to clean it up. I'm really sorry.'

'No, it's not that. Please, I really have to sleep right now. I'll tell you everything okay?'

Vicky agrees, takes him to the bedroom and he lies down, hoping to catch some sleep. At his blindside, Vicky strips completely naked. She calls him, he turns around and sees her completely unclad but he's uninterested and looks away. She doesn't give up though.

She joins him in bed and says lustfully, 'I know this will get you out of the bad mood.'

Tada tells her he's not interested but she still persists, loosens his belt and pulls his shorts down. Her beautiful body unclad breasts are at full glare yet, he looks glum.

She realizes he doesn't even have an erection. He tries pushing her away but she holds her ground, grabs his dick and begins to suck on it. She successfully gets him an erection, sits on his dick and begins to fuck him.

She knows he's not enjoying it but she continues to ride for half an hour until she gets to the peak and experiences a shaking orgasm. She screams pleasurably and he pushes her off him. She checks and realizes he didn't get even a single ejaculation. Now she's certain something is really wrong with Tada.

Per the police's request, at 5pm, Pastor Mrs. Stones arrives at the police station along with Pastor Jenkins and Rev. Drinkwater who are associate pastors of their church. Pastor Jenkins and Rev. Drinkwater are asked to be seated while Pastor Mrs. Stones is taken further in to an office to write her statement.

She is given a pen and a book in which she writes the following:

'It was around 7:50am when my husband was shot. He was shot twice but I can't tell who it was. We had an argument with our son the previous night and we crushed his party. They fought in the morning but I can't say whether my son shot him or not.

I don't believe he did. He asked me to call for an ambulance and so I did. After the ambulance arrived, they drove him to the hospital where he was operated on. Moments later, I was told he's fallen into coma.'

To the police however, the statement isn't concrete and conclusive. It looks fishy and is definitely hiding something. They query her in order to churn out more details. One of the sergeants leads her to the interrogation room where she's met by Detective Burke – the detective assigned to the case.

'Good evening madam, I'm Detective Burke. Accept my condolences for your loss.'

'Good evening, detective. Thank you.'

'I'll like to go straight to the point. Where was your son when your husband was shot?'

'When I realized my husband had been shot, I run to his rescue. I was willing to take as many bullets for him and possibly die, if not in his place, together with him. My son was running away but it could mean anything. It doesn't mean he shot him. Right now, I just want him to recover so he can tell his own story.

'I find your answers baffling. Your answers mean you were present at the scene. However, you claim you don't know who shot him. Would you find it difficult recognizing your own son in broad day light?'

'No.'

'As it stands now, if nothing changes in your statement, you'll have to be arraigned before court as the prime suspect and the only available witness.'

'It's okay by me.'

'Madam, we'll call it a day. I'll meet you again for another round of interrogations and I can only hope you adopt a more positive approach the next time.

'Thank you, inspector. I bear no grudge at all. Thanks for trying to help.'

She joins up with her colleague pastors, they walk out and enter their car. Just as the engine is ignited, Rev. Drinkwater receives a call from the hospital. The news: Bishop Stones had passed away a few moments ago. The time of death was 5:45pm.

Elsewhere, Vicky wakes Tada up around 6pm for supper. He forces him to go rinse his mouth, wash his face and come sit at table with her. Tada sits at table with her but tells her he has no appetite. She begins eating however and tells him she would be offended if he took in nothing.

Yet, Tada doesn't bulge. She stops halfway through the meal and asks him to tell her what's up with him. He gets up from the chair and walks into the bedroom. Vicky takes a last bite at the chicken and follows him. She meets sees him seated on the bed and she joins him.

'Talk to me Tada. You know I'll be of help.' She says, gently stroking his occiput.

Tada bursts out into tears and tells his tale. She springs up to her feet; shocked; worried; terrified.

'What!' she says, 'No, tell me you don't mean this Tada. You shot your dead? Have you gone insane?'

She sits down again, a bit further away from him, and asks 'What happened? Did he survive?'

'I don't know, I fled instantly.' He said in a sober tone, sinking his head into his palms.

'What were you thinking?' She asks with tears in her eyes.

'I don't know Vicky. I took in some heroine that morning, was so angry and I kept the gun in my back pocket to threaten anyone who would stand in my way. I remember it wasn't loaded. I just don't know how.'

'Oh, please cut the crap. You pulled the trigger.' She rebutted furiously.

'Yes I did, but it wasn't supposed to be loaded. I was so high on drugs but it's still too mystifying. The gun wasn't loaded.'

She stands up again, wanders about the room for some minutes and then takes her seat again.

'Tada, the police could be searching for you right now. I'm sorry but you would have to leave.'

'Vicky, where else will I go? Who else would I go to? It's you who's closest to me among all the girls.'

'Do you realize what you're asking me to do? You expect me to house you in here. If the police come searching and find you with me, I'll be held as an accomplice.' She says sternly.

'Vicky, you are asking me to leave? Please give me some days to figure this out, okay? Please.'

'No Tada, I'm really scared. I can't risk going to jail with you. I'm sorry but you'll have to leave.'

She takes her phone, Tada's heart beats – he thinks she's going to call in the police. Then she says, 'Can you please dial your mom's number?'

'What for?' He asks.

'We need to know what happened to your dad – whether he survived or died.'

He dials the number and she calls. Rev. Drinkwater answers the phone of the mourning lady. Vicky speaks to him and asks about the fate of the Bishop. Rev. Drinkwater breaks the news to her. She hangs up and throws the phone onto the bed.

'Your dad died about an hour ago' she says bluntly.

Tada looks so miserable and isn't able to utter a single word. She pities him but has to say what she's got to say. She tells him she's sorry for him but he would have to leave very early the next morning. She even chooses to spend the night in the hall than by him because she's so disgusted at him.

OLD FRIENDS ARE THE BEST

CHAPTER 3 –

The next day is a Sunday morning. Tada had endured a very stressful sleepless night and by 5am, he washes down, dresses up and packs his luggage to leave. He gets out of the bedroom and makes his way towards the hall. Vicky is lying down in a three-in-one couch and pretending to be asleep. He leaves a note by her side and as he leaves, she stealthily opens one eye to watch him.

Tada leaves without having any idea where he is headed. He picks a cab, and after asking the driver about any cheap low profile place he could lodge in, the cab driver suggests Colorado Springs Travelodge. He checks in at Travelodge and sees a number of newspapers on the receptionist' counter. One of them has the headline 'BISHOP KILLED BY SON OR WIFE?' He picks it up and since he's taken in nothing for the past day and was beginning to feel dizzy, he orders for breakfast.

Food is served him but he's able to eat just a little

As James rests in the room, he hears the sound and music from nearby churches and he remembers how beautiful his childhood days were. He misses it so much but now, he's such a mess. The very person that influenced him negatively, Vicky, is the very same person who's betrayed him and given up on him

Meanwhile, that same morning, Pastor Mrs. Stones has very interesting information for him and is trying to reach James but his line is not going through. It's because, right after fleeing the house, he wrote out a few contacts and confiscated his phone.

The day passes so quickly and it's evening. He thinks of what to do and where to go next. He decides that to avoid or delay arrest, it would be best if he left Colorado. He assesses his options and after making a decision, he books a flight for the next day.

He makes a call from a phone booth the next morning, sets off to the airport and flies from Colorado to Oklahoma. He is picked up at the Will Rogers World Airport by Julian Ross who takes him in to her apartment.

Back in high school, Julian Ross was his best friend. They were classmates and most often, James helped her with a lot of the coursework. During the hard times, when her parents' marriage was hitting the rocks, Tada was her main source of comfort. Knowing how much good Tada had done for her, she always felt indebted to him and would relish any opportunity to repay him.

After high school, however, her mom relocated to Oklahoma and she followed suit. Though they'd been keeping in touch with each other throughout the years, they haven't been as close as they were. But one thing they are certain of is that they could trust each other through thick and thin.

Julian is so excited to see Tada after that many years and takes him to her apartment. Julian's apartment is made up of a kitchen, two bedrooms, a hall and balcony. Tada has barely spoken a word since the pickup, is very moody and she knows that's unlike him. She asks him to talk to her and he assures her he would let her in on all the details after he has taken some rest. She agrees.

Tada wakes up at 1pm and Julian has made lunch already. She has absented from work because of Tada. They dine together and after they're done, while sitting at the hall, Tada tells his story.

Julian is shocked, dumbfounded, worried and scared. She knows James has changed from the cool well-mannered good guy she had known to a highly uncultured Casanova but it never crossed her mind this once that Tada could be involved in drugs and guns. She is so disappointed and disgusted. She gets up from the sofa with tears in her eyes, walks into her room and locks herself up, leaving Tada alone by himself. He's worried, scared and remorseful as he sits in the sofa with his jaw in his palms and tears trickling down.

Around 3pm, the bell rings. Tada is awoken by it, so is Julian. He gets out of the sofa and hurries to his room while Julian gets out of bed and walks towards the hall. It's Sam – her boyfriend – who stands behind the door. She opens the door and jumps at him, bending her legs around his waist. He catches her, hugs and kisses her.

He slams the door behind him with one hand, carries her to the sofa and lays her on the back. He kisses her more passionately and untucks three buttons from her shirt. She is braless. He squeezes her tits. She moans loudly but then ceases his hand, pushes him off, sits up and buttons up. He sits by her, holds her hand and asks if she is alright. She says she's just not feeling for it and that all is well.

She wants to tell him Tada, her very good friend, is around and would stay for a while but she doesn't. Sam wants to stay around for much longer but Julian tells him to leave, that she's moody and wants to spend some time alone. Sam isn't happy about it but has no other choice than to leave. He leaves. She locks the door and sits at the hall.

Moments later, Tada comes out and joins her at the hall. She forces a smile at him, but he's unable to smile back. No one says a word until Tada does after about five minutes.

'I'll leave tomorrow morning. I don't want to burden you.'

'No, you don't have to. I never said you were a burden. I'm just disappointed and shocked.'

'Obviously, I am gonna be a burden. Like how you drove your boyfriend away because of me.'

'No James, you shouldn't say that. We'll stick together. You were always there for me, I've to be there for you too.'

'If the police begin searching for me, you could be implicated too. I can't risk that.'

'No James, please stay. At least for the time being. You're more secure here than anywhere else.'

He bursts into tears, Julian migrates from her seat to his and consoles him.

'Everything is gonna be okay.' She says.

She has Tada's head on her laps. He sobs bitterly while she comforts and cuddles him. She recollects those nice times with James at high school when she was on the receiving side of consolation and coaxing.

Oh, how she loved him then. She would relish living those years over and over again. Moments later, she walks Tada to his room and they fall asleep in each other's arms.

Sam has called Julian several times via phone but there's been no answer. At 7:30pm, he returns and rings the bell. Julian is awoken and so is Tada. He tells her to go check but she says she's not expecting nor willing to entertain any visitors. The bell rings the second, third and fourth time but her stance is unchanged.

Sam calls her phone once more but it's on the floor at the hall and she doesn't hear it. He hears the phone ring from the hall yet there's no response. He tries again and again but there's still no response. He is curious and worried. He has a spare key to Julian's apartment. He pulls it out and unlocks the door. He enters and closes the door behind him. He sees the phone on the floor and suspects something is wrong.

He walks stealthily towards her room, opens the door, scans the room and then the bathroom but it's empty.

He g walks towards the other one, opens the door and sees them lying on the bed in an embrace. They are startled, look in the door's direction and see Sam standing there with a shock on his face.

He turns around and begins to walk away. Julian springs out of the bed and pursues him. She stops him midway through the hall.

'Sam! It's not what you think. He is just a friend, my best male friend.' She says desperately.

Sam refuses to look at her. He is so pissed and doesn't want to say a word.

'I'm not cheating on you, I swear it. I was only consoling him. I swear.'

He looks at her with so much disdain and says, 'You still have the guts to lie even when I've caught you red-handed?'

'What did I do?'

'Didn't I just see you lying in bed with a guy?'

'Sam, just lying together, nothing more.' She said frustratingly.

'Oh I see. And you're braless beneath your shirt? Why am I even having this conversation?

'Look Sam, just sit down so we talk okay?'

'What is there to talk about?'

'You should trust me, Sam. I know you do.'

'And you know I'm not blind.'

'Alright but please sit down and let's chat. Give me a chance to explain and you can leave afterwards.'

She tries holding his hands but he withdraws them arrogantly and makes his way to the sofa. Julian speaks, Sam refuses to look at her but she continues. She tells him the guy in there is the childhood friend she had spoken about some time ago, that his dad had died from a gunshot, his mom held as the prime suspect by the police and he himself a suspect on the run.

Sam disbelieves the story until she shows her the newspaper Tada had brought along. However, he tells her to keep a distance from Tada, that he still doesn't like that they had to be lying in bed together. She asks that Sam meets Tada and stays a while longer but he refuses and leaves.

CHAPTER 4 –

Two weeks later, the case is handed over to the judiciary. The Denver Criminal Court commences the hearing of the case. Pastor Mrs. Stones and her son are the prime suspects.

Trial begins and lasts for about three months. Pastor Mrs. Stones takes full responsibility of the murder, accepts the charges levelled against her, is convicted of aiding and abetting murder or attempted murder, and is sentenced to 20years imprisonment.

A month passes since her sentence. Julian and Tada hear of the unfortunate news but he can't go to see her because he's still on the Wanted List and has never stepped out of Julian's apartment.

Julian visits the lady pastor alone on behalf of Tada. She tells her Tada is really remorseful over all that had happened and wants to turn himself in. She also makes known to her the fact that living with the knowledge of having murdered his own dad was too much a burden for him and was weighing him down.

However, she forbids him from doing so.

She tells Julian to tell him not to give up yet, that his dad came back to life about five hours after he was confirmed dead only that he is still in coma. She says to her to tell him that the church is still praying for his dad and hopefully, he'd recover. All she asks of him is for him to turn a new leaf and pray for his dad too.

She returns to Oklahoma and it's a Sunday. She's gladdened by what she's heard. She tells James everything and they all are very happy. Tada feels so relieved that his dad has not died by his hands – at least, not yet.

Julian tries to inform Sam that she's arrived a day earlier than she'd planned but she can't reach him on phone. She leaves sets off to see her beloved Sam.

She arrives at Sam's house at 4pm and rings the bell but there's no one home. She opens the door with a spare key, locks it from inside and pulls the key out because she wants to surprise Sam. She makes her way to his bedroom, freshens up and lies on his bed in her pink panty and bra.

Sam returns home at 6pm with another lady but Julian doesn't notice because she's already sleeping. He lets her in, shuts the door and throws her into the sofa at the hall. He switches on the sound system, opens the volume loudly, returns to the lady and they begin to make out in the chair.

Julian is awoken by the loud music. She gets out of bed and begins to walk towards the hall.

From a distance, she can see Sam busily sexing a lady in the couch. He's so excited and is sweating all over but they don't see her.

She runs back inside, puts on her clothing and begins to make her way out. Upon reaching the hall, Sam sees her and springs up to his feet. The lady gets up as well and begins to dress up hurriedly.

To her utmost disdain and shock, she's a very good friend of hers – Viola. Sam stands in her way to obstruct her but she gives him an unpleasant slap on his left cheek, pushes him to the ground and walks out, slamming the door behind.

Julian is so disappointed and heartbroken. She's always been faithful to him. She feels so betrayed by her friend, Viola – the very friend she would always take a bullet for. She arrives home at 7pm and walks straight into her room without saying a word to Tada who opened the door. He senses something isn't right. He locks the main door and pursues Julian to her bedroom. He sees her lying sideways on the bed, her head on a pillow and a second pillow tightly clutched to her chest.

He sits by her on the bed and notices she has a glum look and is sobbing. She turns her back against him.

He asks if something is wrong but she bursts into tears instantaneously. He pats her back and shoulders softly, telling her to cheer up and that everything would be alright.

Moments later, she turns toward Tada. She has a sad countenance and tears all over her face but Tada signals a smile at her. She pushes his back to the bed, sits over him and kisses him. He's utterly shocked and doesn't kiss back. She notices he's not kissing back so she withdraws the kiss while still sitting on him.

'What are you trying to do?' He asks worriedly.

'What I should have done years ago. Now would you?'

'No Julian, what's going on with you?' He asks suspiciously.

'Really? We'll talk about that afterwards.'

She strips out of her shirt and bra and her breasts bulge out but Tada looks on sheepishly. She takes off her skirt and panty to go completely unclad on top of him. He gets a very strong erection but still has his hands by his sides, refusing to touch. She loosens his belt and unzips his flap. The erection beneath his boxer shorts is so visible at that point.

'Please, I can't let you do this. You're emotionally unstable right now.'

He says in sober tone.

She ignores him and forcefully pulls his shorts and boxer shorts down, his hard-erect dick pops up embarrassingly. He stops her again just when she's about sitting on it.

'Julian, don't make this any harder for me. It's not easy resisting you.'

'Shut the fuck up, okay!' She says sternly.

She holds it and guides it right into her pussy and begins to rock the boat. Tada is shocked and looks on for a while before he begins to fondle her breasts and sexual regions.

They enjoy over an hour of hot sex before they rest. As she lies on the bed, she feels embarrassed after everything but doesn't want him to know. She realizes she's still as shy of him as she'd ever been. However, she's awestruck by Tada's performance in bed. She thinks he is probably ten times better than Sam.

She had been screaming embarrassingly during the session because she just couldn't handle the pleasure. She virtually had to beg Tada to stop before he halted. She thinks it is the best sex she's ever had, that he's a sex beast and she's already addicted to him.

Her phone rings at 9:45pm. It's Sam. She picks up and tells him it's over between them, that he could keep Viola and that she's already gotten a much better replacement. After the call ends, Tada is curious and yet worried.

He asks her and she tells him everything that had happened with Sam. He consoles her but she tells him she doesn't need his sympathy. She jumps onto him again and put them through another session.

While they lay on the bed afterwards, just one thought runs through Tada's mind; he realizes for the first time that the only girl he's ever really loved is Julian. All those other sexual encounters with the numerous ladies had no strings attached to them. This one felt really different.

CHAPTER 5 –

The following day is a Monday morning and it's 8am already. Julian had officially sought permission to be absent from work prior to the trip and was to report formally to work the next day – Tuesday. Just as Tada finishes breakfast and begins to wash the dishes, the doorbell rings. She gets out of bed to check it out and it is Sam at the door.

She opens the door, slaps him in the face, yells at him to leave and slams the door. The door doesn't shut because he has his left foot in the way. He maneuvers his way in and closes to the door behind him. Julian is so pissed that he made his way in. She walks briskly to her room, but, he pursues her there.

She's so enraged and stands at the far corner of her room with her face towards the wall. Sam stands some distance away from her and kneels but she's not looking.

'Julian, please give me the chance to make this right. It's the act of the devil. I swear I never meant to hurt you.'

She doesn't mind him and still has her back turned against him. Meanwhile, Tada has already halted washing the dishes and was eavesdropping from behind the wall.

'Please Julian, we can't end it like this. It was a moment of weakness that I won't let happen again. We've come too far to quit now. You lost your virginity to me and I swear I never touched any other woman. Please forgive me and let's make this work. I can't bear seeing you with any other guy. Just try to remember all we've been through and done together.'

She still has her back turned against him and begins to sob. He gets up and walks slowly towards her, stands right behind her back and plants his right palm into her left palm.

She sobs even more loudly and holds on to his hand. He rests his jaw over her shoulders, his left cheek kisses her right cheek and he says, 'I'm truly sorry. I promise never to hurt you again.'

She turns around and places herself into his arms and weeps in his arms.

She says tearfully, 'I always loved you and did everything to make you happy. Why? Why do you have to break my heart?'

Sam takes her to the bed, sits them down, places her head on his laps and he pats her slowly. Moments later, Tada knocks on the door.

Julian shouts from the bed, 'James? Am I needed?'

'Umm, breakfast is ready.' He says.

'Alright, a moment please.'

He turns away and goes to set the table. Meanwhile, Sam tries kissing Julian but she doesn't settle for it. She asks him to join them at breakfast. He's unwilling to but he does because she insists. Julian and Sam come out of the room and take their seats on the four-seater dining table.

Sam takes his seat right next to Julian. Tada joins them and sits directly opposite Julian. Tada steals a glimpse at Julian as he sits down but she avoids eye contact – she's feeling so guilty and shy about the previous night's experience.

She asks that someone prays but no one is willing. She feels too guilty and sinful to pray, Sam feels too hypocritical to do so after being caught the previous fay, and Tada has not said a prayer in years. Since no one opts too, Julian does guiltily.

"Father, we pray and ask that you forgive us and sanctify this meal. Amen."

They respond AMEN to it. Julian takes the ladle and serves them custard with bread and fried egg. They start eating but Julian isn't able to look Tada in the face for even a second, Sam and Tada are still not cool with each other, and so there's silence for a while until Tada speaks.

'Hey, does it taste good?' Tada says, looking straight at Julian.

'Yes, it is.' She says with a nervy tone, still avoiding Tada's eye.

He smiles at her while Sam looks on enviously. Tada realizes how uncomfortable he's probably making the lovers feel. He finishes up quickly and excuses himself. Tada walks into the kitchen but moments later, Sam joins him.

'Hey you, it's about time I faced you man for man.' Sam says, tapping Tada's chest provocatively.

'Dude, get your hands off me. What's your problem?' He says hesitantly.

'Look guy, I don't know why but I've never liked you. I see the way you look at her. Don't even dare to mess up with her. I swear I'll kill you if you ever screwed my girl.' Sam says sternly.

'Oh really? So, you know that, and you screw someone else's girl right?'

'Screw you, nigga! I've made myself clear enough.' He says, pointing his forefinger in his face.

Julian walks in, beholds the scene and asks what's happening but Sam is quick to say it's nothing. He walks towards her to assist her with the plates she's carrying while Tada walks straight into his room.

Julian sees Sam off around 11:30am. She closes the door, walks towards Tada's door and knocks. He gets up from the bed and opens up She asks to see him in the living room rather than in his bedroom. They sit in the sofa and Julian still struggles to look him in the face.

'I'm sorry for last night. My emotions got the better part of me.' She says shyly and embarrassedly.

'You think last night was a mistake? You regret it?' He asks worriedly.

'Yes James. I was so hurt and I wanted to do something to hurt him too but I really love him. I can't believe I did this to him.'

'Really Julian, so everything was about him? The person didn't really matter but the act? I don't matter?'

'What are you saying James? He's still my boyfriend.'

'No, he's not... He wasn't last night. You made him.'

'James, can we please put this issue to bed?'

'I know guys like that. They are very cunning yet the least faithful.'

'James! Please stop it! Stop it okay? Don't tread on this line again. Please don't make this any more difficult for me. Let's forget about last night.'

Tada nods disappointedly in agreement.

During the weekend, Sam makes his way to Julian's apartment around 10am. She's never let him make love to her since the incident that occurred a week ago. Julian lets him in. Tada is seated at the hall but upon seeing Sam who looks into his face distastefully, he gets up and walks into his room.

Julian is worried. She has always wanted his boyfriend and best friend to be cool with each other but in the past week, their relationship has been more polarized than ever. She sees some hatred and jealousy in Tada's eyes that she'd never seen before. It seems to have awoken after that sexual intercourse they had.

Now that she feels so guilty, she can't even put herself in the shoes of a mediator. She knows how angry Sam will be if he finds out about what had happened between them. She really doesn't want to lose the guy she lost her virginity to.

They spend hours at the hall chatting and romancing but she's a bit uncomfortable throughout. She doesn't allow any more than a shallow kiss from him. He's worried by her demeanor but she explains that, after what she saw, it's gonna take some time for her to recover and trust him again.

But Sam has one request. He's beginning to feel very uncomfortable about Tada's presence, he's growing increasingly suspicious that he could try something stupid anytime and he proposes that she makes him leave. She says she can't do that but he tells her she would have to make a choice to clear any suspicions he's been having.

He explains that it was one of the reasons he fell for Viola's advances, that he'd begun to fear and suspect something fishy was going on between she and Tada. In order to keep her boyfriend, she assures him that he would do something about it.

ROUGH TIMES AREN'T EVIL TIMES

CHAPTER 6

Julian has a talk with Tada and tells him it'll be good for both of them if he got a place of his own but she doesn't know Tada had overhead her conversation with Sam.

He's disappointed that Julian chose to betray their longstanding friendship and memories just because of a boyfriend who is not worth it. Within a few days, he finds an occupied apartment a couple of blocks away and moves out.

He says to her, 'Thanks friend. You took me in and had my back when I sorely needed it. It's the same thing I always want to do for you.

One thing I can assure you is that I would die for you anytime, the very thing your guy would never do for you, not even once.'

She cries as he leaves and tells him she's sorry things had to be that way but she loves Sam and doesn't want to ruin the relationship. She hugs him for minutes before letting go of him. She goes with him to see the place which is just a walking distance away. The apartment has just one bedroom, a hall and a kitchen.

They take his bags to the bedroom and she asks, 'Why did you have to choose a place so close by?'

He shakes his head and says, 'It just was available and I took it.'

'Can I stay and help you set up the place?' She asks guiltily.

He walks towards her, faces her, takes her hands and says, 'Look me in the eyes and tell me you don't love me.'

She looks away and declines to answer.

Tada speaks, 'After what happened, I realized where my heart really was, who I'd ever truly loved. You're all I've ever had. I'm sorry for all the things I did in the past but I'm trying to be a changed person now.'

Tears begin to flow down her eyes and he continues, 'For a sexually active person like me, I'd not had any sex in months. Yet, I never bothered to touch you, all because I love you and never want to hurt you. I know you love your boyfriend but think of it; who do you love most? Who makes you feel more complete?'

She sobs more intensely; Tada grabs her head and kisses her softly. She kisses back more intimately and just when she's about to lose control of her urges, Tada withdraws.

He tells her she has to be leaving. She bows her head shamefully and Tada walks her to the door. She turns around, kisses him again and tells him she wants to save her relationship.

Later in the day with some minutes past 7pm, someone knocks on the door, his heart thumps. He's not mingled with society for the past four months and in the least, he has no friends. He wonders if it could be the police but the person knocks again. He decides to open up and meet whatever fate awaits him. He opens the door and standing before him is a cute pretty lady holding two shopping bags.

'Hello' she says.

'Hi'

'Umm…, my name is Tasha. I guess you're my new neighbor. I'm the occupant of the apartment next to yours.'

'Okay, nice' He says hesitantly.

'Actually I have a little problem and I was hoping you could help.'

'Oh, really?'

'Yea. But you look nervous, can I at least come inside?'

'Okay, sure' He says hesitantly.

She moves in with her shopped items.

'Oh, your hall isn't set up yet? Nowhere to sit then.'

He scratches his head and explains that he just moved in and has to do some shopping first. She also explains to him that she went shopping and seems to have lost the keys to her apartment and the spare key is locked in the apartment. She tells him she just needs a place to pass the night and that she would figure out something the next day. Tada doesn't decline to help.

She stashes her stuff – which are food ingredients – in the kitchen and joins up with Tada in the room.

'Your kitchen isn't stocked, not even a burner. You've taken nothing in for supper?' She asks.

He scratches his head again and stammers, 'Umm…, I'm not that hungry.'

'Really? Can you cook at all?'

'Well, not really.'

'Ok, but you kinda look familiar. I'm trying to recall where.'

'Me? No, we've not met.' He says, turning his face elsewhere. He's scared that perhaps she's asking because she'd seen his face in the newspapers for the negative reasons. She sits on the bed, holds his jaw and tilts his head towards her face. She stares him right in the face but he can't look into her eyes.

'Oh, it's you. I remember where.' She says excitedly.

'It's who? No, I'm not him.' He rebuts ferociously.

'Do you realize you didn't even tell me your name?'

He thinks swiftly about a name to use. He knows his name was used in the newspapers and he has to forge a name. He uses his nickname since it is an unofficial one.

'I'm Tada.'

'Exactly! You're the one.' She says excitedly.

Tada is confused, looks at her and asks, 'Which one?'

'You're Tit Tada. I was in the same college with you. I really and really know you.'

'Oh my God' He says, slapping his palms into his face.

'Can you do me one extra favor?'

He pulls his face out of his palms and says, 'What do you need?'

'Can you please not touch me tonight?' She says wryly.

'Come on don't be ridiculous.'

'Look, I mean it. Okay?'

'Alright, but for the records, I never forced any girl or maneuvered any. They all asked for it and sometimes when I declined, they just wouldn't let me be. Besides, I'm not the same person anymore for these past few months.'

She looks at him doubtfully and then suddenly, there's a knock on the door again. She notices the shock on his face and asks him if she should check for him. He agrees.

She opens the door and it is Julian. Sam, who has been tracking Julian to find out Tada's new place, is spying from a corner but they can't see him.

'Hello' Julian says, 'is the guy there?'

'What's your name, please?'

'It's Julian.'

'Okay, give me a minute.'

She informs Tada. He comes to meet her at the door and lets her in. Now, Sam sees him and is certain that is Tada's new place. Since Tasha is in the bedroom, Julian decides they should go to the kitchen and talk. She tells him she's come over because she feels lonely. She enquires jealously about the girl in his room but he explains everything to her. Julian tells him to spend the night at her place then, so he wouldn't have to be with the girl, but Tada refuses.

He reminds her that Sam doesn't want him to be there and that she'd already consented to that request. They spend about an hour together; she hugs him affectionately and leaves.

He enters the bedroom and realizes Tasha is bathing and singing passionately. He lies on the bed. Moments later, Tasha dries herself up and walks out of the bathroom completely naked – She didn't notice Tada had come in. Tada unintentionally beholds her fully unclad body and his eyes are almost fixated permanently on her. She notices Tada is in there, she screams and makes her way back to the bathroom.

Tada walks out again and settles in the kitchen.

He returns minutes later and finds her lying on the bed. She's put on one of his shirts which covers her upper body and just a few inches beneath her bottom. Tada lies by her. For over five minutes, no one says a word. Tada does first.

'I'm sorry for the incident.'

'Just shut up! What you did wasn't the least honorable. You got what you wanted right?'

'Seriously? I didn't plan that. I didn't know that was gonna happen.'

'Of course you did. You meet a girl for the first time and you manage to see her nudity against her wishes, that's really disgusting of you.

He continued to argue out his innocence but she wouldn't hear him out. Tada is pissed that she's accusing him wrongly, gets out of the bed and walks into the bathroom to wash down. Minutes later, he dries himself up and walks out completely naked. Tasha looks in his direction and sees everything.

She screams and turns her eyes away, covering her face with a pillow. Tada puts on his pajamas and joins her in the bed. She's so pissed at him and asks him why he had to do that. He tells her it was the same thing she had done and yet had accused him for the outcome. She apologizes to him and he apologizes too.

With some minutes past 11pm, Tasha shuts her laptop after completing a movie. Tada isn't asleep either though he was virtually doing nothing.

She turns towards him and asks, 'Are you waiting for me to sleep so you do your thing?'

'What thing? Look, I told you I'm not the same person anymore. Besides, I've never in my life forcefully or persuaded any girl to have sex with me.'

'Oh really? Not the same person anymore you say but I know that even today being your first night here, a lady came to see you. She was probably here for it.'

'Come on, stop being ludicrous. Does she look like that kind of lady?'

'Whatever! I just don't trust you.'

'Well, trust isn't a cheap commodity. But do you even realize for a second that you're lying down on my bed braless and without any panty and that alone would turn any guy on?'

'What?' She quickly checks the level of the shirt and pulls it further down. 'What did you see?'

'I saw nothing. I just know that no decent lady will wear the same panty she's worn during the day at night. Besides, I can smell your pussy from here.'

She knocks him and asks him to stop talking. He stands up, pulls out a pair of shorts from his wardrobe for her to put on. She puts them on and they chat throughout the night. She tells him she knows of the crime he's committed and recognized him immediately he saw him.

She also tells him that she's had a crush on him since the first she saw him on campus, when he was a good kid, but could never make any advancement towards him. She tells him she doesn't believe he's responsible for the shooting and wanted to hear it from his own mouth.

More importantly, she lets him know that she is a good Christian girl, a virgin, and that's why she was so furious at him for seeing her nakedness. She informs him that she's still attracted to him even as they spoke.

She asks him to have faith in God that He will forgive him and listen to his prayer. As she speaks about God with him, he breaks down into tears, confesses all his sins and prays to God to forgive him, take his mom out of jail and heal his dad. By 3am, they begin to feel sleepy. She kisses him on the forehead and they go to bed.

CHAPTER 7

They wake up early in the morning and she lets him know she still can't believe how she made it through the night without being seduced by him. They laugh it off and she tells him she's off to prepare them breakfast at her place.

There's a knock on the door at 7:30am. Julian is already in there because she wants to see him before she reports to work. Tada thinks it's Tasha returning with breakfast. He opens the door excitedly only to behold the unexpected – Three police officers at his door.

Two point their rifles at him while the other asks him to place his hands over head.

He turns around, they cuff him, and search his apartment. Julian is shell-shocked at what she's seeing whiles Tasha hears them and rushes out only to see him being taken away. With tears in her eyes, she runs towards him to speak with him but they obstruct her. She runs back at Julian who's still not gotten out of the room.

'Julian, I swear I'm not responsible for this. Did you? Please no, don't tell me you did.' She says tearfully.

'I know it wasn't you but I know who did. Don't worry.' She says in a bitter tone.

She picks her bag, walks out, and then returns to Tasha again.

'Tasha, do you love him already?'

She nods unashamedly and says, 'I do.'

She turns about and sets off again but Tasha pursues her.

'What are you gonna do? Will you follow them to Colorado?' Tasha asks tearfully.

'Yes, but I've something to deal with now. I'll leave later in the day.'

'Let me come with you. Please wait for me.'

Julian who's in a haste to go finish up what she's got to do pulls her business card out of her bag, hands it to Tasha and says, 'Give me a call in the afternoon.'

Tada is flown straightaway to Colorado. Meanwhile Julian anonymously gives the police intel about Sam's dealings. They search Sam's house and find three unregistered guns, bags of marijuana and heroin in his basement. They arrest him right away and lock him up in a cell.

In the afternoon, she joins up with Tasha and they set off for Colorado. Julian leads them to visit Pastor Mrs. Stones at the prison to inform her that James had been arrested. Before they speak out, she has good news for them that her husband had recovered from coma the night before. She's very excited but is saddened after hearing Tada had been arrested.

They leave for the police department where Tada is being kept and they are given five minutes to speak with him. Tada speaks more religiously and inspirationally than ever before; he tells them to cheer up and that God is in control.

They're gladdened by his words of encouragement yet saddened by his impending condemnation.

Three days later, Tada is arraigned before court as the second suspect but next to him is a third suspect, Louisa. She arrived a day ago at the police station and said she'd a confession to make. She's a friend of Tada's who was at the party. She says after having been embarrassed twice by Tada's parents during the two parties, she was pissed off and decided to kill them. She claims she was under the influence of marijuana that morning when she did but after months of seeing an innocent mom suffer in prison and her son on the run for a crime neither had committed, she couldn't live with the guilt anymore.

The hearing is adjourned to the following week. The Bishop is discharged the next day and he passes by the prison to see his beloved wife. They encourage each other. He's accompanied to the house by Pastor Jenkins and Rev. Drinkwater.

The following week, the court resumes the case. The Bishop testifies and his wife is brought out of prison to re-testify. The judge passes his verdict; Pastor Mrs. Jones' sentence is quashed, James is sentenced to three months' community service and Louisa is sentenced to 20 years in prison.

The Bishop pleads the cause of the young lady, arguing that she'd actually repented of her deeds, shown remorse and obviously wouldn't repeat it. The judge and the jury agree with him but cannot let her go unpunished. The sentence is reduced to 8years in jail and 2years community service.

The family returns home along with Julian and Tasha. It's obvious from James' speech and actions that he's turned a new leaf and his parents are so impressed. He apologizes to them and thanks them for staying strong for him through all those trying times

They hug each other and say a prayer of thanksgiving to God. They climb upstairs, leaving the three youngsters at the hall.

James doesn't know what to say to them. He kneels and thanks them. Julian stands him up from a kneeling posture, stares him right in the face – wanting to kiss him but unable – then hugs him. She kisses him on his cheeks and he kisses her on the forehead. Tears drip down her eyes as she hugs Tasha and whispers in her ears, 'I won't stand in your way. If you really love him, he's all yours.' She walks into the backyard, leaving James and Tada alone at the hall.

Tasha sits right by him on the sofa, grabs her hand and says to her, 'You're a perfect woman. You deserve an excellent man.'

'People may know you as Tada, but I'll always know you as James and James is a great guy. I love you James.'

She kisses him on the cheek but he grabs her head and gives Tasha her first ever passionate kiss. It feels like heaven on earth.

I like to write great romance stories that take you on an emotional journey whether tears, laughter (or both) or just steamy hot fun (or all of them).

Please... let me know if you had enjoyed this great story

THANK YOU ☺